THIS OLD
BAND

written by
TAMERA WILL
WISSINGER

illustrated by
MATT
LOVERIDGE

Sky Pony Press • New York

With a **clang clang boodle bang**,
Play the sky a song.
This old band plays all day long.

Number ten
Plays **tug tug**.
Ten plays **tug tug** on a jug.

With a *Pug pug boodle bug*,
Play a cowboy song.
This old band plays all day long.

Number nine
Plays **ting ting**.
Nine plays **ting ting** with a string.

With a *ping ping boodle bing*,
Play the ranch a song.
This old band plays all day long.

Number eight
Plays *click click*.
Eight plays *click click* with a stick.

With a **tick tick boodle pick**,
Play a mustang song.
This old band plays all day long.

With a **foam foam boodle bome,**
Play the sage a song.
This old band plays all day long.

Number six

Plays **SCOOT SCOOT**.

Six plays **SCOOT SCOOT** with his boot.

With a **shoot shoot boodle loot**,

Play a bison song.

This old band plays all day long.

Number five
Plays **dub dub.**
Five plays **dub dub** on the tub.

With a **rub _rub boodle bub_**,
Play the rocks a song.
This old band plays all day long.

Number four
Plays *far far*.
Four plays *far far* on guitar.

With a **gar gar boodle bar**,
Play an eagle song.
This old band plays all day long.

Number three
Plays *tell tell*.
Three plays *tell tell* on the bell.

With a **nell nell boodle ell**,
Play the pines a song.
This old band plays all dusk long.

Number two
Plays **knock knock.**
Two plays **knock knock** with a block.

With a
tock tock boodle lock,
Play a mesa song.
This old band plays all night long.

Number one
Plays *shoo shoo*.
One plays *shoo shoo* on kazoo.

With a *foo foo boodle boo*,

Play the kids a song.

This old band plays all night long.

This old band, ten through one,
Played and now they're almost done.

With a clang clang, tug tug, ting ting, click click,
home home, scoot scoot, dub dub, far far, tell tell,
knock knock, shoo shoo . . .

TOODLE OO!

Play the stars a song.

Sky Pony Press books may be purchased in bulk at special discounts for sales promotion, corporate gifts, fund-raising, or educational purposes. Special editions can also be created to specifications. For details, contact the Special Sales Department, Sky Pony Press, 307 West 36th Street, 11th Floor, New York, NY 10018 or info@skyhorsepublishing.com.

Sky Pony® is a registered trademark of Skyhorse Publishing, Inc.®, a Delaware corporation.

Visit our website at www.skyponypress.com.

10 9 8 7 6 5 4 3 2 1

Manufactured in China, December 2013
This product conforms to CPSIA 2008

Library of Congress Cataloging-in-Publication Data is available on file.

ISBN: 978-1-62873-595-6